Rufous the Fox

We can judge the heart of a person by the way they treat animals.

Neil Cheesman

In this wonderful story, you will go on a captivating journey following the courageous fox Rufous! Through twists and turns he finds himself lost and alone... What follows is a heartwarming tale of bravery, resilience and friendship as Rufous tries to find his way home.

Immerse yourself in the pages so beautifully written by author Neil Cheesman and you will witness the power of friendship and loyalty and an insight into the world that foxes face every day.

Kevin Newell
Humane Wildlife Solutions
humanewildlifesolutions.co.uk

Profits from sales of the book will be donated to:

The Fox Project
Registered Charity No. 1190070
Tel: 01892 824111

Established in 1991 as a specialist Wildlife Information Bureau and Fox Deterrence Consultancy, the Fox Project have additionally incorporated a Wildlife Hospital which admits and treats over 1000 foxes per year, including over 300 cubs.

The Fox Project appears regularly on TV, radio and other media, both in the UK and internationally. They have received awards from the RSPCA, International Fund for Animal Welfare, media and TV.

Chris Packham and Anneka Svenska are Patrons.

https://www.foxproject.org.uk/

Find a Wildlife Rescue Near You

https://helpwildlife.co.uk/

Set in the English countryside, this is the story of Rufous, a young fox who, after escaping from a pack of hounds, finds himself transported far away from where he was born.

This is a tale of courage, compassion, and survival with Rufous desperate to find his way home. Accompanying him on his perilous journey is a vixen called Piccola.

The story portrays life from the perspective of a fox, together with interactions with other animals that can talk and communicate with each other, in a world that is unknown to humans.

Perils along the journey include a wide fast-flowing river, a railway track, fox hunters, hounds, and more.

Table of Contents

Chapter 1

Rufous the Fox Explores

It was a sunny autumn afternoon, where fluffy white clouds moved slowly across the blue sky, like sheep grazing on a vast open landscape.

Rufous was exploring the part of the valley that was called 'Wild Meadow', so-called due to the vast number of wild plants and flowers that grew there. It was a few weeks since he had left the sanctuary of the den by the old chalk pit where he was born. He missed his brothers and sisters, who he used to play with every day, but he was no longer a cub and felt the innate need to explore.

Rufous paused to taste a juicy low-hanging blackberry on a dense prickly shrub.

As he nibbled away, a chirpy Robin hopped onto the top of the blackberry bush and called out confidently, "Hello Fox, do they taste nice? The ones at the top are really lovely."

Rufous looked up at the little red-breasted bird and replied, "Hello Robin, yes these are lovely, thank you."

The little Robin decided now was a good time to taste the biggest blackberry that he could see. He wasn't disappointed. It would help to give him much-needed energy for the forthcoming winter.

"Sometimes," said the Robin, "the bigger ones don't taste as nice as the smaller ones, but this one is very yummy."

"Hm," replied Rufous, "I'm not sure - they all taste good to me!" as he gulped down another blackberry.

As the Robin looked at Rufous he started to laugh and chirp.

"Why are you laughing?" asked Rufous, curiously, as he nibbled away at another blackberry.

"You have blackberry juice all over your whiskers, and it looks funny", said the Robin.

As Rufous looked up at the Robin he chuckled and said, "Yes, and you have blackberry juice all around your beak!"

They both laughed together as they set about eating some more blackberries. While the little Robin continued hopping along the top of the shrub, Rufous searched around the lower edges of the large bush.

After a short while, the little Robin paused eating as he felt compelled to sing. He flew up higher and perched on a small branch that was overhanging the blackberry bush and with his red breast proudly displayed, sang a brief but tuneful song which caused Rufous to stop eating and listen. His long ears twitched as he wanted to hear every note. Rufous noticed that all of the other birds nearby had stopped to listen.

When the Robin stopped singing he hopped back down to the bush.

"Did you like my song?" he asked.

"It was really lovely," said Rufous. "I am sure it could be heard far away!"

"Thank you," said the Robin, "I have to let others know that this is my territory."

"I see," said Rufous. "You must have a very big territory!"

"Yes, I do," said the Robin proudly. "I have to sing lots of times every day, especially early in the morning at the dawn chorus. I don't usually like any visitors, as they are usually after my food, but you won't be able to reach the blackberries high up, and you seem friendly, so it is okay for you to stay."

Rufous smiled and replied, "Thank you. You have very beautiful red feathers on your chest?"

"Thank you," chirped the Robin, feeling even more proud, and deciding now was a good time to eat a small insect that was crawling over a leaf.

"There must be lots of other birds and animals in your territory," Rufous commented. "Isn't there enough food and shelter for everyone?"

"Well," said the Robin, "to be honest, we do all live fairly happily together as there is enough food for all of us, and if there are any predators about we do all shout out to warn each other. But, sometimes I do have to let them know that it is my territory."

"I see," replied Rufous, somewhat distracted as his senses told him something was wrong, very wrong.

Suddenly, a male Blackbird flew excitedly through the trees sounding its alarm call loudly and repeatedly. From its orange-yellow beak, the alarm call sounded: chook-chook-chook!

"Danger, danger,' called the agitated Blackbird as other small birds in the woodland also started sounding their alarm calls.

Rufous then heard a sound that he had heard only a few times before but he knew it always meant danger and often led to the death of a fox. It was the sounds of short sharp notes from some instrument that the humans blew into and then the distant sounds of hooves from many horses, and then the sound of dogs barking. Rufous knew that he had to run for his life.

Small birds flew to the tops of trees while small mammals hid in the undergrowth. A few rabbits that were nearby scurried into their burrows – they feared the sounds and their hearts were racing.

In a single moment, after hearing the Blackbird's call, Rufous was running - away from the baying dogs and the humans on horses - he ran along the edge of the woodland and towards a hedgerow that he could see in the distance across a meadow. His heart was pounding while his legs ran as fast as they had ever run before. He didn't know this part of the countryside very well and he hoped that he would find a way through the hedgerow - and being down a slight slope, maybe there could be water beyond which he could use to hide his scent.

The barking dogs and the humans on horses blowing their horns sounded closer and Rufous knew that he had to find cover and fast. The hedgerow was less than 50 metres away and Rufous was breathing hard - he scanned the hedgerow for an escape route but he couldn't see a way through. Without looking behind him he felt sure the chasing dogs could now see him as their barking had become frenetic.

As he neared the edge of the meadow, Rufous could now see what looked like a 'rabbit run' under a metal fence, it was small but he hoped he could escape under it. As the barking dogs got closer he ran forward and squeezed under the fence, the sharp metal spikes digging into his back didn't stop him, and he was soon into the shrubbery. As he crawled through the dense undergrowth he could hear the dogs at the fence where the hole was too small for them - he hoped it would take them a little while to find a way through, but he couldn't be sure so he scurried on as fast as he could.

The hedgerow was thicker than he had hoped and he felt his fur get entangled on some brambles and the sharp thorns stabbed his skin.

As he fought for a way through, he became aware of dogs barking to his right. There must have been another gap in the fence which he hadn't seen. Having struggled through the dense vegetation, he could now see daylight.

The dogs to his right seemed much closer.

Finally, Rufous leapt forward into a wide open space that stretched out to his left and right. His feet landed on sharp stones on which there were a pair of railway tracks - he knew this was a dangerous place to be but at the moment it was less dangerous than the hunters behind him.

To his left, Rufous saw the black carriages of an old freight train. He ran towards them hoping they might give him some shelter from his pursuers. He could hear the dogs barking and now the sounds from the humans were more of anguish. He ran alongside the black carriages and looking up he saw that they had openings in the sides. The barking hounds were much closer and he could now also hear the sound of their feet on the stones behind him.

Rufous had to make a decision, try to outrun the hounds or outwit them. Choosing the latter, he leapt into the opening in one of the carriages. As he did so he felt the floor he was standing on start to move and he had to steady himself otherwise he would have fallen over.

He realised that the large manmade box he had jumped into was moving - the sound of the barking dogs was now getting quieter. He had changed one danger for another.

As Rufous looked out of the opening he saw the countryside passing by - slowly at first and then faster - he contemplated jumping out but he considered he would most likely injure himself on the sharp stones. He turned around to see what else was there but as his eyes adapted to the darkness he realised it was empty apart from some old sacks in one corner. He decided to go and lay down on the sacks and rest until it was safe to leave his temporary home. With the rocking to and fro and feeling very tired he soon fell asleep.

As time passed, and daylight turned into darkness, the movement stopped and it caused Rufous to waken. He walked slowly towards the opening of the carriage and looked out - there were many other railway carriages as well as some buildings. He realised that this was a place where many humans would be. Suddenly, he heard voices and he knew that he had to move quickly – he saw a wooden fence nearby with some broken panels and he leapt into the darkness towards it.

At this moment Rufous didn't know where he was, but he did know that he needed to find his way to woodlands and green fields. That was where he felt at home. He hoped that on the other side of the fence, there would be a field but when he crawled under it he was startled to see many twin sets of bright lights on cars to his left and his right - they were going faster than

anything he had ever seen before. The sounds were lou
to his ears as they passed by - he watched partly
mesmerized before deciding that he had to cross in
between these manmade monsters with humans inside
them. On the other side of the road, he could see a
hedgerow and some trees beyond it.

He watched and waited for the right moment -
now was the time to run across the hard ground - and h
ran as fast as he could...

Chapter 2

Rufous Meets Piccola

As Rufous ran across the hard surface, he felt his senses heighten in fear for his life as the human machines were loud and very fast and were heading straight for him - but he managed to get across safely. On reaching the grass on the other side of the road he breathed a sigh of relief - he saw an opening in the hedgerow ahead and dived through it.

He now found himself on the edge of a small copse. Although he could still hear the sounds of the human machines, he felt somewhat safe as he ventured forward across the soft woodland floor. The trees and plants around him had a familiar smell to them and it reminded him of home.

The first thing that Rufous had to do was to find somewhere to hide and be safe, that he could use as a base from which to explore, before trying to figure out how to find his way back home.

As Rufous crept through the dark woods, searching the shadows with his keen eyesight, there were no sounds of other animals, just the distant sound of cars on the road behind him.

There were many big tall trees, most of them were old and Rufous could smell the moss that was growing around the base of them.

Suddenly, Rufous heard the screech of a Barn Owl and then seconds later, another owl called a reply. It comforted him to hear the owls as it reminded him of home. And it meant that animals were able to survive in this woodland.

Ahead of him, he saw a huge old tree that had fallen down, and creeping nearer he saw that the base of the tree had unearthed a large amount of soil, creating an opening under the roots. He couldn't smell the scent of any other animal so he investigated the dark space.

Crawling into the darkness, Rufous discovered that it was big enough for him. It was also quite dry. This appeared to be an ideal place to retreat to and be safe. He sat down and pondered what to do next.

Rufous believed that he could find his way home by looking at some of the brightest stars in the sky at night and also by where the sun rose and set in the sky. His wise father had taught him the ways of the world, and finding your way around by looking at the sky was one of them.

While returning to the place of his home was his underlying aim, the first thing that Rufous needed to do was to find some food to give him energy for the long journey ahead. He might have to stay here for a day or two but then he would start his quest.

Having had a short rest, Rufous began to explore. He set off through the woods, making a mental note of the track that he was using.

Although he had a very good sense of smell, he couldn't find anything to eat as he meandered through the woods in the darkness. However, he soon found himself at the edge of the wooded area with buildings ahead of him.

From stories that his father had told him, it was possible to discover various types of food that appeared to have been thrown away by humans. Sometimes, the food was just lying on the ground, but other times in a bag or a bin, which had to be knocked over for the contents to tumble out. It seemed like a fairly lazy way of getting food as it meant that he wouldn't have to run around to hunt or search for some ripened fruit. But, it might save him some energy, if he could easily find something to eat.

Rufous stepped out from the shadows of the woodland into a half-lit track that humans used - the ground felt hard under the pads of his feet. He looked left and right and started exploring the area. There were no humans around at the moment but his senses were on alert as from what his parents had told him, some humans were friendly while others could be very aggressive towards foxes.

As he walked cautiously but swiftly along, he moved from shadows to lit areas – the street lamps seemed like bright yellow stars on the top of tall branchless trees.

In one of the shaded areas close to where humans lived, Rufous spotted the black shape of a full bin bag placed against a wall. His mother had told him that these bin bags often had many different things hidden inside them - and sometimes food! She said that often, i was difficult to get inside where the edible contents might be, but on this occasion, there was a hole where Rufous could put his snout - he sniffed carefully - and sure enough an aroma found its way to his nose.

Although he wasn't sure what it was, or exactly where it was, he started rummaging amongst various smelly objects until he found the remains of a human's meal. Rufous didn't understand why humans would throw away food - maybe they just had too much. In the world of the fox, there was never too much to eat, either in one go or to cache for later consumption. Although he wasn't too keen on some of what he was eating, most of it was quite tasty. He ate undisturbed for several minutes, constantly lifting his head to look around to make sure he wasn't being observed.

When he finished eating Rufous explored some more, moving silently along the footpaths and roads. As he turned around a corner he found himself at the entrance to a cul-de-sac and near the end of it were four humans who were shouting and waving large sticks in the air. He was about to run past when he realised that trapped by the humans was a cowering fox.

With their large sticks raised in the air, the humans were getting closer to the fox and there was no means of escape.

Without thinking about it, Rufous ran behind the humans and barked as loud as he could, and as they turned in surprise he shouted to the trapped fox, "RUN!"

The trapped fox seized the opportunity and ran past the humans who were looking at where Rufous had barked from, which was in shadows, so they couldn't see him.

Rufous turned swiftly around and the two foxes sprinted away together as fast as they could. The humans had been caught off guard but they were soon chasing the foxes waving their sticks and shouting angrily.

Rufous shouted at the fox, "Follow me, I know somewhere we can hide."

Although foxes would usually be able to outrun humans, it was apparent that Rufous' new friend was injured and couldn't run as fast as they would normally be able to.

As they ran along the road, from one shadow to another it was clear that one of the humans was catching up on them.

"We have to keep going," said Rufous, who was trying to encourage his injured friend. "I am trying, but my leg hurts," replied the vixen.

Suddenly, from somewhere in the dark sky above, came the sound of "KEWIK, KEWIK", and a large Tawny Owl swooped down at the human, who stumbled and fell over at being surprised in such a way.

The owl called out to the foxes, "There is an opening in the hedge after the next light, jump in there and you will find a track".

"Thanks," Rufous called back.

As the two foxes reached the gap in the hedge they heard again, "KEEWIK, KEEWIK". As they dived into cover, Rufous glanced back and saw the brave owl flying above the human and then away into the darkness.

As the two foxes crept further along the darkened pathway it led into woodland. All was quiet behind them.

They walked in silence, both aware that the quieter they were, the safer they would be.

After a short while, Rufous, who was leading, paused. He sniffed some vegetation to his left. "I know where we are. I walked along here earlier and left a scent. It isn't too far where we can hide and be safe."

Rufous started walking again along the narrow track, a track that was used by animals and most humans wouldn't even know it was there. The injured vixen followed him.

Seemingly from nowhere, a dark shadow flew silently through the air past them and landed on a tree just above the pathway.

"You made it then," said the Tawny Owl.

"Yes," replied Rufous, "thanks to you. That was a very brave thing to do".

"It was nothing, really," replied the owl, "humans can be very cruel. Some of them seem to want to hurt animals for no reason."

Rufous considered what the owl had said and he replied, "Yes, you are right."

"I have to go now," said the owl. But before she could fly away into the night, Rufous asked her, "What is your name?"

The owl looked surprised, as not many animals had asked her what her name was. "My name is Tawzel."

"Thank you for helping us, Tawzel", said Rufous. "Yes, thank you very much," said the vixen by Rufous' side.

"My pleasure," said the owl, and she flew silently away into the night.

"There is somewhere for us to hide just along here," Rufous said, as he headed towards the base of the fallen-down tree that he had discovered earlier. "In here," he said quietly as he crawled into the dark space, where there was just enough room for the two of them.

"We should be safe here for a while. What is wrong with your leg?" he asked.

The vixen replied, "One of the humans threw a large stone at me and it hit me. It hurts but I think it will feel better very soon."

She continued, trembling slightly in the darkness "Thank you for helping me. I was trapped and wouldn't have escaped from the humans without your help. I don't think it is safe anywhere around here. They will come for us soon."

"I think we will be safe for tonight," Rufous said in a reassuring tone. "We can rest for a while before deciding what to do."

"By the way, my name is Rufous. What's yours?"

"Piccola," replied the vixen.

"Hi Piccola," Rufous said, "let us get some rest."

"Hi," Piccola replied, already feeling tired and ready for sleep after being chased by humans.

After a few minutes, Piccola was asleep. Although Rufous was tired, he felt that he needed to stay awake and be alert just in case they were followed or tracked. The silence of the night, with the occasional call of an owl, comforted Rufous as he lay next to his new friend. He wondered when he would start his journey back home but he now had someone that he needed to protect. He wasn't sure what he was going to do as he drifted into a half-asleep state.

Chapter 3

Finding Food

Having been woken by the dawn chorus, Rufous and Piccola had emerged from their makeshift den and were stretching their legs beside the old oak tree. A melodic Robin was singing nearby while a blackbird was also trying to compete to be one of the earliest risers.

As Rufous sniffed the air he said, "I think it will rain today." The dark grey clouds above appeared to agree.

"How is your leg this morning?" he asked.

"It feels much better, thanks," replied Piccola.

"We should try and find some food before too many humans are about," said Rufous.

"I know somewhere. Follow me," said Piccola, as she turned and headed down the track they had walked down the night before. Piccola's limp seemed to have gone.

After a short while, they were back on the road where they had been chased, but this time they went in the opposite direction. It was early in the morning and there weren't any humans about, although they could hear some human machines in the distance. They walked along the roadway a short distance and then Piccola turned right into an alleyway, and then she immediately turned left into another narrow path, which was quite muddy. It didn't look like many humans had walked along here in quite some time.

Ahead of them was a row of small conifer trees that had grown close together side by side, making an evergreen hedge. Piccola crept in between two of the trees, saying to Rufous as she did so, "Be very quiet."

The smell of the conifers was quite sweet and Rufous couldn't help but sniff the trees as he crept through.

On the other side of the trees, there was a low wall and before Rufous had a chance to speak, Piccola had jumped onto the wall and then down onto a lawn. Rufous followed cautiously, feeling apprehensive as they were both standing on short grass with a building only a few metres in front of them. Most of the house was in darkness but in one place there was a light shining from within. Rufous could hear human voices, although they sounded different in some way, somewhat quiet and excited.

"Quickly," said Piccola, "over here." She led Rufous over to a much smaller wooden building. Next to it on the ground was a metal bowl containing food.

Piccola sniffed it cautiously before saying, "It's okay to eat." And she started eating.

Rufous stood for a moment, still unsure as to whether it was not only safe to eat but was it safe to be there. He felt he could trust his friend so he ate alongside her.

After a few minutes, they had finished the food and Piccola said, "It's time to go." And she turned and ran towards the low wall and the conifers. When Rufous reached the wall and was about to jump over it he heard a noise behind him. He didn't turn around, but following Piccola, jumped over the wall and out between the conifers.

"I guess that is one of the kind humans," said Rufous.

"Yes, I think so," said Piccola, "They leave food out every day."

"I think we should go back to the den now," Rufous suggested.

"Yes, okay," Piccola agreed.

On their way back to the den they didn't see any humans. Overhead, the grey clouds continued to get darker.

Once inside the den, where there was just about enough daylight to see each other, Rufous explained to Piccola what he had to do. He described in detail his lucky escape from the humans on horses and the dogs chasing him and his long journey in the box that travelled on metal tracks.

"The thing is," Rufous continued, "I know I was lucky to escape with my life, but I felt at home in the countryside where I was born and I would like to see my family again, even though we didn't seem to get on very well and everyone wanted their own space.

"I feel I need to at least try to get back home. I can follow the stars and the sun in the sky to find my way."

Rufous felt that he had been talking for a long time and Piccola had said nothing, and she looked sad.

"Where is your family?" Rufous asked.

"My family are all dead," replied Piccola.

"I am sorry," Rufous replied.

"They were killed by humans with dogs. They hunted us down and although we split up, they still managed to catch my family. I was lucky to escape. I saw one of my brothers being torn apart by several large dogs. It was awful."

"I'm very sorry," said Rufous, not knowing what else to say.

They both fell silent, each with their head lowered.

Outside of the den, it started to rain. As the gentle sound of raindrops landed on leaves the melodic sound of birdsong quietened. A rumble of thunder in the distance indicated that a storm was on its way. Many animals in the natural world would be taking cover.

As Rufous and Piccola huddled together in the relative dry of their den, they heard a dog barking in the distance, and then another. It wasn't clear whether the dogs were getting closer or if they were just imagining it, but the two foxes started to become fearful.

Just as Rufous was about to suggest that they move and run, the rain started pouring down and a crack of thunder overhead caused the ground to vibrate. The dogs stopped barking.

The rain became torrential and drops of water started to fall onto the foxes, but not enough for them to worry.

Rufous voiced his thoughts, "When I leave, will you come with me?" he asked, hoping for a positive reply.

Piccola had wanted Rufous to ask this question, "Yes, I would like that. We can look out for each other. I have nothing to stay here for."

"Then we will leave tonight," said Rufous. "If it continues raining I doubt we will be able to see the stars in the sky, but we can start by following the metal tracks that brought me here."

"Okay," said Piccola.

They both sat in silence before they fell asleep while they listened to the rain falling and the thunder occasionally growling overhead. The storm continued until just after dusk.

The silence of the evening woke them.

Rufous was the first to speak.

"I think we should mostly travel at night when it is dark, there won't be as many humans around and we should be able to stay safe. Shall we go now?"

"Okay," replied Piccola.

They left the makeshift den for the last time and then immediately sniffed the air to see if they could smell any danger. There was none.

There were puddles of water everywhere and they both stopped at a fresh-looking one and had a drink.

Rufous looked at Piccola and said, "Okay, let's go," and they both headed off down the pathway through the woodland that Rufous had first arrived on.

As they walked quietly along, the skies above started to clear and a few stars could be seen.

Suddenly a voice startled them. "Hello, where are you going?" asked Tawzel the owl, who was perched in a tree above them.

"Hello Tawzel," replied Rufous, just being able to make out Tawzel's silhouette against the night sky. "I need to find my way back home and as Piccola doesn't feel safe here she is coming with me. We are heading to the metal tracks and will then head in the direction where the sun rises."

"It isn't safe here for any animal," said Tawzel in a sad voice. "The humans keep cutting down the trees and taking over all of the fields. There is hardly anywhere for me to hunt anymore. And this small piece of woodland is the nearest for quite some way."

"Maybe you would like to come with us?" asked Rufous, cocking his head to one side.

"Hm," replied Tawzel, "I will have to think about this. Although it is hard to survive here, I was born her it is where I know. If I decide to come I will find you along the metal tracks. Right now I need to find something to eat."

In one swift movement, Tawzel flew away into th night, announcing her departure with a loud "KEEWIK

Rufous and Piccola paused for a moment and the continued on their way. They first had to cross the bus road and then on to the railway station. The two foxes were both anxious and excited at the prospect of their journey and what lay ahead of them.

Chapter 4

The Journey Begins

As they crept through the hedgerow near the road, the two foxes could see the immediate danger that lay ahead of them. Hidden by the undergrowth, they stopped to look. Although it was dark they could see that there were humans inside the cars that were travelling along the road. On the front and back of the cars, there were lights of white and red. The cars moved very fast and it would be a matter of life and death crossing the road without getting hit.

"I'm frightened," said Piccola, "I have seen what they can do."

"We will wait," replied Rufous reassuringly, "when the time is right we must both run together and very fast, without stopping. When I say 'go', follow me."

"Okay," replied Piccola, who was feeling uncertain, "if you think we can make it."

They sat waiting and watching for several minutes until there were no passing lights to be seen.

"Go!" Rufous said loudly, and they both ran across the road as fast as they could. As they got halfway across Rufous could see two bright white lights in the distance to his left that were getting closer very quickly, but they kept running and through the hole in the wooden fence on the opposite side of the road.

When they got to the other side of the fence they stopped, pausing in the shadows and letting their eyes get used to the darkness in front of them. There were several railway carriages stationary on the metal tracks. On either side of the tracks, there were jagged stones and also a small strip of rough grass and undergrowth. The tracks went west to the left and east to the right. In the distance to the left, two humans seemed to be talking to each other, oblivious to the two foxes.

Rufous paused for a moment and then looked at Piccola and said, "Follow me. If we see or hear any humans we have to go into the undergrowth and hide until they have passed."

"Okay," replied Piccola, "that sounds like a good plan."

Rufous led the way as they started heading east.

The route alongside the metal tracks was in darkness and Rufous and Piccola had to tread carefully to avoid the sharp jagged stones underfoot. They had only gone a few hundred yards when the metal tracks started to make a vibrating sound.

"Quick, hide in there," said Rufous and they both darted into the undergrowth, hiding out of sight.

As they stood still they watched as a train and carriages rumbled past them - it was like thunder right next to them and it made their bodies vibrate.

After a few seconds, which felt a lot longer, the noise had gone and it was quiet again.

They crept cautiously back close to the track and continued walking. Apart from taking cover several times to avoid the noisy human machines, they managed to find scraps of food along the way.

With the sky above having cleared of rain clouds, there were several bright lights in the sky and one particularly large one.

The landscape by the side of the metal tracks had now changed and there were fields on either side.

As they considered whether to stay close to the tracks or head down into a field, the decision was taken for them. The pathway disappeared and the tracks went straight ahead across a large metal bridge with a high drop on either side.

They stopped, sniffed the air, and listened. They could hear the sound of water as well as smell the scent of it in the air.

"It's a river," said Rufous. "It will be too dangerou to cross on the tracks, as there is nowhere to escape. W will have to go down into the field and swim across."

Rufous led the way down the steep embankment and they crawled under a wire fence. They both looked out towards a wide expanse of pasture and walking a short distance to their left, found themselves on the bank of a large fast flowing river.

"This looks almost as dangerous as walking across the bridge," said Rufous. Maybe we need to wait until daylight before we think about swimming across."

"Yes, I think so too," replied Piccola.

"Maybe we should take cover in the hedgerow until it gets light?" suggested Rufous.

Before Piccola could reply, there was the sound of "KEEWIK!" from above. Suddenly, Tawzel flew in from above and perched on a fence post.

"Well, here you are!" she exclaimed. "You have travelled quite some way. I thought the water might slow you down."

"It's good to see you," said Piccola. "We have decided to rest here for the night, but in the morning will you travel with us?"

"Yes, I will," said Tawzel, "but you cannot stay here. There is a human in the next field walking this way and he has a long stick that makes a loud sound like thunder and it kills animals from a long way away. I have seen it before. You will have to cross the river tonight."

"Can we not hide near the railway tracks?" asked Rufous.

Tawzel paused for a moment before replying, "He has a large light that shines a long way. If the light shines on your fur then you will surely die."

"Then we will have to swim across the river now," said Rufous, looking at Piccola.

Before flying off in the direction of the human, Tawzel said, "I will see where the human is, maybe I can distract him. I have never seen them hurt an owl before, so I think I will be safe."

"Take care," said Rufous and Piccola in unison. They then turned and walked over to the water's edge.

The lights from the stars and the sky partially lit up the vast stretch of water and the far bank looked a long way off. The river flowed under the bridge and the sound of a waterfall on the other side of it whispered 'danger', echoing under the concrete arches of the bridge.

"We will have to swim against the current," said Rufous. "We don't know what is under the bridge as it is too dark, and it sounds like the water is falling on the other side."

"Yes," replied Piccola, "let's go."

"Stay close," Rufous said.

"I will try," replied Piccola.

They both went into the river and each with their head, nose, back, and tail out of the water they started swimming towards the safety of the far bank. They got a short way out when they realised how strong the current was and they had to adjust their swimming to stop them from being swept away downstream.

It was hard work but after a short while, they were almost at the middle of the river where the current was at its strongest.

From above them they sensed rather than heard the sound of a bird flying - it was Tawzel.

"You need to hurry," she called to them. "The human is in the field where you were and he is shining his light. If he shines it across the river he will surely see you."

"We are going as fast as we can," gasped Rufous.

Tawzel flew away into the darkness back towards the human.

Although Rufous and Piccola were swimming they were silent in their movements. The only sounds that could be heard were the ripples of the fast-flowing river. Although it was the middle of the night, there was a small amount of light from the stars and moon above, not enough to see details but enough to see shapes in the darkness.

Suddenly, a noise from the darkness behind them - the sound of a human walking across the field - as much as they tried, humans couldn't walk quietly.

Rufous heard the human on the riverbank behind them, they were breathing heavily. Suddenly, there was a bright light shining out across the river, it hadn't foun its prey but it carried on searching.

Rufous knew that if they carried on across the current of the river, then they would be seen.

"Stop swimming now!" Rufous whispered firmly t Piccola who was alongside him.

"But, the current will take us under the bridge and onto the waterfall..." replied Piccola.

"Stop now!" repeated Rufous, as Piccola started to overtake him. "Start swimming again as fast as you can when you get under the bridge."

But it was too late, as at that moment a bright light shone on them.

As the current swept them toward the darkness beneath the bridge, Rufous heard a sound. It was the clicking sound of the human's thunder stick. He expected to hear thunder and be killed any second.

From close to where the human was standing came the loud sound of KEEWIK, KEEWIK – which echoed across the water. For a moment, the light moved away from the foxes as the human lost his balance, due to Tawzel flying very close to him, calling as she did so. The human shouted something and then began scanning the water again with the light. Just as the light was about to reveal Rufous and Piccola, the two foxes reached relative safety behind a large concrete archway under the bridge.

The current that was moving them along seemed to be getting stronger. The noise of the falling water was getting louder.

"Swim now!" Rufous barked. The two foxes put every ounce of energy into their efforts.

After a few minutes, they had escaped from the clutches of the main flow of the river and were in shallow calm water. With tired limbs, they crawled out of the water onto the grassy bank. Having shaken most of the water off themselves, Rufous said, "We can rest for a few minutes, but then we will have to get away from here and find cover for the rest of the night."

"Yes," replied Piccola.

As they commenced their journey, the meadow that they found themselves in was full of the scent of wildflowers, with oxeye daisy, knapweed, bird's-foot-trefoil, and sweet vernal grass amongst others growing.

It didn't appear to be managed in any way by humans, so it seemed a fairly safe place to be.

As they moved swiftly away from the river, they followed close to the embankment that contained the metal tracks. At least they knew they were going in the right direction.

Having reached a suitable distance from the river where they felt safe, they came across a particularly large area of tall grasses. They crept into the middle of it and lay down on the soft vegetation. They licked themselves clean before both falling asleep, tired from their efforts and needing energy for the day ahead.

As Rufous and Piccola were in that half-asleep state, they were both comforted by the distant sound of "KEEWIK, KEEWIK".

Chapter 5

Trapped

The two foxes slept well into the next day, waking occasionally to search nearby for food and water. They concluded that it was best to rest as much as possible during the day and then travel further at night, but this wasn't always going to be possible. When the sun had reached its highest point in the sky, the two foxes heard the sound of humans walking along the gravel by the side of the railway tracks. Rufous and Piccola sat up and listened intently. Although the humans were some distance away, it wouldn't be long before the two foxes might be visible to them.

"We can either stay here in the long grass hiding or we can go on. What do you think?" asked Rufous.

Piccola thought for a moment before replying, "They might not mean us any harm."

"But you can never tell with humans," replied Rufous, "they feed you one day and kill you the next, I don't understand them."

"You are right," said Piccola, "let's go before they see us."

The foxes crept slowly through the long grass until they reached the edge of the field where they entered woodland, consisting mostly of pine trees. The carpet floor beneath the tall trees was covered with several years' worth of pine needles and cones that had rotted away. The scent of the pine trees filled the air.

As Rufous led the way with Piccola close behind, she said to him, "I hope we find some food soon, I am starving."

"Yes, I am hungry too. I am sure we will find something."

They meandered through the trees for quite some time, constantly alert, until they came across a narrow human track, one that would be used for walking on.

They stopped and looked in both directions. There were no signs of humans.

Rufous sniffed the air - just the smell of pine cones.

"The track doesn't look very well used," said Piccola quietly.

"No, it doesn't," replied Rufous.

"It might lead us to where humans are and there might be some easy food," continued Piccola.

"Yes, but it might lead to danger," Rufous replied.

"But I am starving," said Piccola as she dropped her head.

"Okay," replied Rufous, as he turned to the right and started walking quickly along the pathway, "but if we see any humans, we must hide quickly, back into the woods."

Piccola followed without saying anything, hoping that they might soon find some food. There wasn't anything edible on the ground in the pine woods.

After they had walked a short way along the narrow track, the scent of food reached their noses.

"Can you smell that?" asked Piccola, lifting her nose in the air and sniffing.

"Yes, I can," replied Rufous, also drawn to the scent of something edible.

"It smells like something humans would eat," continued Piccola, as they both started walking in the direction of the aroma.

"Yes," replied Rufous, "we must be very careful."

As the pathway meandered left and right they found themselves in a clearing in the wood. The humans seemed to have cut down several trees and had left some things that belonged to them

The aroma was now much stronger.

They both stopped and scanned the area ahead with their keen eyes.

"I don't like it," said Rufous, "we must be very careful. I can't smell any humans here now - I can't see them and I can't hear them, but I don't feel safe here."

"They have probably gone now and discarded some leftovers here," replied Piccola.

They both crept slowly around the area, with their senses on high alert.

"Look," said Piccola excitedly, "over there!"

Rufous looked at the large piece of food that the humans had left. It smelled and looked very tasty, but something didn't seem right.

The piece of food was inside a small wire container, just lying there.

They crept closer and studied what was in front of them.

"They must have left it here by mistake," said Piccola. "It looks very tasty."

"Something is wrong," said Rufous. "I think we should go. We can find something to eat somewhere else."

"But it is here, right in front of us," Piccola pleaded.

"We must leave it and go," snapped Rufous.

"I can't," said Piccola, creeping slowly into the container and biting into the piece of food.

At that moment a spring-loaded piece of metal slammed down shut behind Piccola, trapping her inside the cage.

Piccola seemed to be unaware of her predicament as she eagerly chewed the food in front of her.

Meanwhile, Rufous scrambled around the outside of the cage frantically trying to see if there was a way out.

"It's a trap!" Rufous shouted at Piccola, "There's no way out!"

Suddenly, Piccola came out of her trance-like state and realised what had happened. She screamed inside of the metal meshed cage.

"I am sorry," she cried, "I should have listened to you, but I was just so hungry and the food smelled so good. I couldn't resist it."

Piccola crept down in fear, looking about her waiting to see what would happen next.

"I can't see any way out," said Rufous, as he scampered around the cage containing his trapped friend.

He used his teeth to grab part of the trap that had dropped down but it wouldn't move.

"I'm sorry Piccola, I can't find a way out," said Rufous.

"What will they do with me?" asked Piccola.

"I don't know," replied Rufous, fearing the worst, but not saying what he thought.

Piccola cowered down and shivered.

Rufous could feel his heart pounding, ready for action, but not knowing what to do.

At that moment there was the distant sound of two men talking to each other and walking towards them.

"You have to go and hide," said Piccola.

"I won't leave you," replied Rufous.

"You have to go," pleaded Piccola. "Maybe there will be another time to help me."

"Yes, maybe," replied Rufous reluctantly. "I will hide, so they can't see me, but I will come back for you."

"Okay," said Piccola. "Go now!"

Rufous looked around and saw that a short distance away there was some thick undergrowth where he could hide. With the voices getting closer he ran and hid there, lying as low as he could.

When the two men came into sight and saw Piccola in the cage, they raised their voices in excitement. They went over to the cage and started to kick it, maybe hoping for a response from Piccola. They were rewarded with a snarl from her. They both laughed.

The two men spoke with each other and the taller of them walked over to a metal container. Rufous saw the man take something out and go back to the trap, where he then poured some water into an opening which went into a small bowl. A small piece of food was also thrown in.

Rufous looked on curiously. He had feared the worst when Piccola was trapped but now he didn't understand what was happening. They had trapped Piccola but were now feeding her. Did they intend to keep her?

The two men looked carefully at the trap, and having spoken with each other they turned and walked away along the same pathway they had arrived on.

Rufous waited until he couldn't hear the humans anymore and he cautiously crept back to where Piccola was trapped.

"How are you?" Rufous asked, "Did they hurt you?"

Piccola looked up and answered, "I am okay. They have given me some food and water. I don't understand what they want or what they are going to do with me."

"No, I don't know either," replied Rufous.

Rufous scratched around the edges of the cage but could find no way in. The metal structure was far too strong. He tried again in several places using his teeth, but it was no use. He only ended up getting a bloody jaw where he had been scratched by the metal.

"It's no use, I can't get in."

"I can't see any way out," said Piccola, as she scratched and clawed around the inside of the cage. When finally conceding defeat she lay down with her nose pressed against the wire mesh, with her eyes looking pleadingly at Rufous.

Rufous lay down next to the cage and pressed his nose against the cage until he could feel Piccola.

They lay together like this for some time until hunger pangs started to make Rufous restless.

"I have to go and find some food," said Rufous. "I will also have a look around to see if I can find where the humans are.

"Okay," replied Piccola. "Be careful."

"Yes, I will," said Rufous, as he got up and walked through the undergrowth to find some food. He glanced around and saw that Piccola was watching him leave.

"I'll return as soon as I can," Rufous called out as he glanced back toward Piccola.

"Okay," replied Piccola hopefully.

With a heavy heart, Rufous left his trapped friend. Although knowing that he would return he was unsure how he would be able to rescue Piccola.

With his head and heart full of anguish, he searched for food during the remainder of the day, and on into darkness, grabbing snacks of vegetation wherever he could. He used the time to explore the woodland and nearby meadows, some of which were soaked in water. He had to walk carefully as in some places it was more like marshland.

At one point, he discovered that there was a river nearby, which -although looking fairly deep - flowed slowly. On it, there were several barges (or houseboats), and on some of these, he could hear humans talking. Rufous could see that each of these floating objects was tied to the bank so that it wouldn't move. As he stood watching he could smell food that the humans were eating.

This made Rufous feel hungry, so he scavenged along the river bank and was lucky enough to find some food that had been thrown away by humans.

"Humans are so wasteful," Rufous muttered to himself as he chewed on some tasty scraps.

After a short while and having eaten enough to satisfy his hunger pangs, Rufous retraced his way back through the darkness to the trapped Piccola.

Rufous could see that Piccola was asleep, so in order not to disturb her, he lay down next to the cage that she was trapped in. He rested for a short while, even managing a brief period of sleep, when suddenly he was woken by a call from some distance away, "KEEWIK".

The sound woke Piccola with a startle, "What's that?" she asked, somewhat confused. Through the darkness, she could see Rufous next to the cage.

"I think it might be Tawzel," replied Rufous.

Rufous called out with a loud bark, and the sound of "KEEWIK", came as a reply.

"How are you?" Rufous asked Piccola.

"I am okay," she replied. "Did you find any food?"

"Yes, I did," said Rufous. "I had a good look around the woodland and meadows. There is a lot of water and also a river with humans nearby. But I didn't see the two that trapped you."

Suddenly, and without making a sound, Tawzel flew onto a low branch just above them. "I found you," she said. "What has happened?"

"Piccola has been trapped by humans," replied Rufous.

Piccola looked sheepishly from Rufous to Tawzel.

"I was foolish," Piccola said, "it was a trap and I didn't see it."

"It's okay," Rufous said, trying to comfort her, "you weren't to know what the humans would do and you were very hungry."

"Trapped by food," said Tawzel, "you won't be the last one to have that happen to them. Humans know the weaknesses of animals. We have to be clever to outwit them. Is there no way out?"

"We have looked and tried but the trap is very secure," said Rufous.

"I am sorry," said Tawzel, "what will you do?"

"At the moment, we just have to wait. Maybe there will be an opportunity to help Piccola escape," Rufous said. "We don't know why they have trapped her."

Tawzel looked down at them and said, "I'm sorry I cannot help you escape. I will keep a lookout during the night and if I see or hear humans coming this way, I will let you know."

"Okay, thanks Tawzel," said Rufous.

"I have to go now, but I will be back," said Tawzel as she flew away silently into the darkness.

Rufous lay back down next to Piccola's cage. They both said nothing through the rest of the night.

Shortly after daybreak, Rufous was woken by the sound of a human walking through the woodland towards them.

"I will go and hide," Rufous said to Piccola, "but I will be watching."

"Okay," she replied, fearfully, not knowing what the human was going to do.

Rufous crept over to the undergrowth where he had hid before and lay down out of sight, watching the footpath entrance and glancing back to Piccola.

After a few minutes, one of the humans that had been there before walked into the clearing, carrying something in their hand. They went over to Piccola's cage and kicked it. When Piccola jumped and snarled, the human laughed.

The human had their back to Rufous so he couldn't see what they were doing. After a few minutes the human left. Walking back the same way they had come from.

Rufous waited until the human's footsteps could no longer be heard and he crept over to Piccola's cage.

Piccola was busy eating something that the huma must have placed into the cage.

"They have given you more food," said Rufous.

"Yes," said Piccola, "it's very tasty."

"Hm," replied Rufous. "I don't like it, I don't trus humans."

"I don't either," replied Piccola, continuing to eat

As Rufous watched his friend eat, he commented "I wish I knew what the humans are planning to do wit you."

Piccola was too engrossed in the food that she ha been given but gave an acknowledging glance to Rufou:

After Piccola had finished eating she had a drink water and then came to the edge of the cage and looked at Rufous.

"What do you think will happen to me?" she aske

"We will find a way to get you out," said Rufous. "We just have to be patient."

They both lay down together for a short while and then Rufous went searching for some food for himself. He returned after a short while and watched over his friend until darkness. No human returned until the following morning when they once again gave Piccola some food and water.

Chapter 6

Escape

This same procedure went on for several days unt
one morning, as the dawn chorus of birdsong filled the
air, Rufous and Piccola heard the sound of humans in
the distance. It was earlier than the previous mornings
and this time they could hear many humans, together
with the sound of several horses' hooves on the ground
along with many barking dogs.

As the two foxes listened intently, they heard the
humans walking towards them along the path. There
were several of them and they were talking excitedly.
Rufous and Piccola knew that the time had come and
they were to find out Piccola's fate.

Rufous wasn't sure what to do. He wanted to stay
and protect his friend but reluctantly he decided to go
and hide in the nearby undergrowth, waiting for the
right moment to come to Piccola's rescue. They might
only have one chance and maybe the element of surprise
was all he had. He waited and watched as the noisy
humans came closer. As they walked into view he saw
that there were four of them and each was carrying a

large stick. He was ready to fight for his and Piccola's life as they neared the cage.

Three of them stopped and one of them walked forward. Rufous was ready to pounce.

The human put down his stick and opened the cage. They shouted something but Piccola was frozen in fear and didn't move. They then kicked the cage which prompted Piccola to run out in the direction of Rufous. As she passed him, Rufous turned and they both ran off. They could hear the humans shouting at them.

Rufous and Piccola ran as fast as they could until they were far enough away from the humans to feel safe. They were panting rapidly as they paused for a brief rest.

"We did it," panted Piccola.

"Yes," replied Rufous, "but they let you go deliberately."

As they both stood there panting Rufous realised what was happening. In the distance, they heard a human blowing a hunting horn, and it echoed across the landscape.

"They are coming for us. Run!" shouted Rufous.

It was lucky for Rufous that he had explored during the previous days as he followed his previous trail through a lush meadow.

What followed was the increasing sound of horse galloping and many dogs barking.

It wasn't easy to run fast in the long grass, even with the slight track that Rufous had previously made.

They ran through a small hedgerow and into the marshland. Piccola made the mistake of running the wrong way and after a few metres was stuck in mud.

Rufous was too late to stop her and called out to her, "No, not that way, you must come back."

As Piccola crawled back through the mud, precious seconds were lost and they could hear the baying hounds getting closer.

"Hurry! As fast as you can," shouted Rufous.

Once Piccola was out of the mud, Rufous said, "Follow me and stay close."

They ran as fast as they could along the narrow pathway through the marshland, but it wasn't easy to go fast. The sound of the hounds chasing them grew louder. The horses seemed to have gone a different way.

While Rufous was running he wasn't sure where they would go once they got through the marshland, as beyond that there was the river and nowhere to hide along the towpath in either direction as far as you could see.

The ground was wet and muddy but at least the tall grasses helped the two foxes to not be seen, although the hounds behind them were getting closer and would soon see them on the winding narrow pathway.

As they reached the towpath, Rufous had to decide which way to go in the hope that they might find some means of escape.

He turned right and Piccola followed him. As the ran along the short grass of the path in the distance ahead of them they could see humans riding on horses coming towards them. Behind them, they could hear tl hounds that were about to come out of the marshland.

Just ahead of them floating on the river was a barge.

"Follow me, jump, and then hide!" shouted Rufous.

He jumped onto the barge and Piccola was right behind him - they then hid under a tarpaulin out of sight.

As they lay hidden, Rufous and Piccola could hea the sounds of the hounds and the horses getting much closer.

The hounds were soon by the side of the boat, barking loudly.

Rufous feared that the hounds would also jump o board the barge, but for some reason, they had stopped

From somewhere on the barge, a human started shouting at the humans on the horses, and they in turn shouted back.

After a few minutes of this, the human on the barge must have untied the barge from the bank as it started moving on the river.

There was suddenly the sound of a noise that seemed to make the barge go faster.

Rufous sensed that the humans on the bank weren't happy, but the human on the barge didn't seem to care as they didn't reply.

For a short while the hounds and the horses ran alongside on the bank, but then they stopped. Loud voices were heard from those on the horses, but it didn't stop the barge.

The two foxes sat in relative darkness, hidden by the tarpaulin. All they could hear was the rhythmic sound of the barge's engine and the sound of the river as it passed by. While they were safe they stayed where they were.

And so time and the riverbank passed by.

Rufous wasn't sure how long had passed but the barge coming to a halt and the engine stopping caused him and Piccola to be alerted. For the moment, they stayed hidden.

They sensed that they were once again tied to the bank. For a short time, they could hear a human moving around the barge but it now seemed like they had now gone.

As if from nowhere, they could smell food.

Rufous couldn't resist the aroma. He poked his head out from their brief refuge to see where the smell was coming from.

"I'm going to look," he whispered to Piccola.

"Be careful," she replied.

Rufous looked out and there in front of him were two plates with food on them. He looked carefully around and couldn't see any humans.

"I think it is okay," he said to Piccola.

Piccola joined him in looking out from their hiding place.

"How do we know it isn't another trap?" she asked him.

"It just feels different," he stated confidently.

The two plates of food were only a short distance from where they had been hiding and by taking a few steps forward they were able to stand next to the plates.

They sniffed carefully. They both looked around but there were no humans to be seen. Rufous glanced to the left and he could see that the barge was tied to the bank.

With their hunger pangs getting the better of them, and believing the food to be safe, they ate it all.

When they had finished Rufous said to Piccola, "It looks like a human left this for us."

"Yes," replied Piccola.

"I don't understand humans," said Rufous.

"No." replied Piccola. "They are strange."

Rufous jumped up and stood on the edge of the barge. He looked along the riverbank and couldn't see a sign of anything.

He jumped back down and said, "I don't think we should stay here. We need to find somewhere away from humans."

"Okay," replied Piccola.

They both jumped up on the side of the barge and jumped onto the grassy riverbank.

As they started to walk quickly away from the barge they heard a human call out to them from the barge.

They both looked around and saw that a human was sitting in the shadows. The man that was sitting there was waving a hand towards them. He looked 'friendly'.

They both turned and carried on walking towards a hedgerow that was ahead of them.

They crawled through the undergrowth and into a meadow where there was another hedgerow that led towards a large clump of trees.

Running alongside the hedge they headed toward the trees where they hoped to find some shelter until dusk.

Having reached the cover of the small copse they found somewhere to hide by the side of a fallen tree.

"I think we will be safe here for a while," said Rufous.

"Yes," I think so too," replied Piccola.

"Thank you for staying to help me," continued Piccola.

"That's okay," replied Rufous, "I am sure you would have done the same for me."

"Yes, I would," replied Piccola.

"We can rest here for a while and explore the area when it gets darker," said Rufous.

Piccola nodded. They both lay down and were soon asleep.

Chapter 7

Exploring

When the sun went down and dusk arrived, Rufous and Piccola woke up refreshed. As they stretche out their legs, they considered which direction to go.

Rufous lifted his nose to the air several times. Th slight breeze was bringing with it some smells that he was familiar with.

"There must be a farm nearby," he said, as he continued to sniff the air. "If we are careful, we might find some food there."

"Okay," said Piccola. "As long as you think it will be safe."

"Let's go and take a look," said Rufous, as he led the way towards the farm that couldn't be too far away. "If it isn't safe then we can stay away."

Creeping out of the undergrowth, they found themselves on an old overgrown pathway that led in the direction of the unknown farm. As they walked slowly and steadily along, dusk turned into darkness.

Ahead of them, they could see a few old farm buildings. Everywhere was in darkness and it all appeared to be deserted. Rufous scanned the area with his keen eyesight and even the building where it looked like humans might live was also in darkness.

They walked in silence towards the ramshackle buildings.

"What is that smell?" asked Piccola.

"I am not sure," replied Rufous, "I think it's coming from inside that old shed over there."

Maybe the smell was a sign that there would be something to eat.

They headed towards the shed but when they reached it they found that the door was closed and they couldn't get in. As they started exploring around the side they could see that the wooden panels were very old and were broken in places. It wasn't long before they found a hole that they could both get through.

They crept through and found themselves in a large dark open space, barely lit by a couple of small lamps. Along each side of the shed there were many cages, stacked several rows high, and inside each of them were chickens. The smell seemed to emanate from the large number of bird droppings that were present in the cages. In the middle of the shed was an old long bench, and on it, there were numerous chicken eggs - neatly placed on egg trays.

Rufous and Piccola crept slowly towards the eggs, and as they did so the chickens realised that the foxes were present and became agitated, fluttering and calling out loudly. Although they were safe in their cages, they were stressed due to a predator being so close.

Rufous and Piccola had no intention of trying to break into the cages and headed straight for the eggs, biting into the shells and eating the contents, one after another.

The noise from the chickens had got louder and Rufous became anxious that it would be heard by humans.

He turned to Piccola and said, "We have eaten enough, we must go now."

"Okay," replied Piccola.

With the incessant noise in their ears, the two foxes made their way back to the hole through which they had entered.

After they had crawled through they stood briefly outside of the shed looking both ways.

Suddenly, from out of the shadows came a large cat - walking slowly but steadily towards them - its eyes fixed on both of them.

For a second or two Rufous and Piccola were frozen in their tracks.

Rufous whispered to Piccola, "Walk slowly away towards the field to our left, when I call out to you, run, and run as fast as you can. I will be behind you."

"Okay," replied Piccola. She turned and walked slowly away.

The feline had stopped, crouched down, and was looking at Piccola and then at Rufous.

The aggressive creature started to hiss at Rufous - and then crawled slowly closer to him.

Rufous could see its large claws.

As the cat looked ready to pounce, Rufous turned and ran as fast as he could – shouting to Piccola as he turned, "RUN PICCOLA!"

Rufous could hear the frustrated creature right behind him, but after a short while, the foxes had outrun the cat, who had stopped in the farmyard - content that victory was his.

They reached a field where the grass was quite long but they managed to find a narrow track that meandered through it.

"Well, that was close", said Rufous.

"Yes, it was," replied Piccola, "but the eggs were tasty."

"The chickens were frightened of us, but they can be happy living in those cages", replied Rufous.

"No," replied Piccola, "it must be awful not being able to run around outside."

They walked on for some time in thoughtful silence.

"Are we heading east?" asked Piccola.

As Rufous looked up into the night sky he replied "I think so."

"I wonder where Tawzel is?" asked Piccola.

"Yes, I wondered that too," replied Rufous.

They walked slowly on into the night before finding somewhere safe to rest, under an old oak tree.

Chapter 8

Danger

Having rested for a short while, Rufous and Piccola began their journey east again. The dark sky above them was speckled with stars, while the moon shone brightly. They walked in silence across many fields, pausing occasionally to rummage for snacks along the way.

Suddenly, the silence was broken with the sound of KEEWIK, KEEWIK", as Tawzel flew above them.

"Hi Tawzel," called out Rufous, "you managed to track us."

"Yes," replied Tawzel, "I have been following you for a while from a distance, but I have to stop to hunt to keep my energy up."

"We stopped at an old farm and have made good progress since then," replied Piccola.

"Yes, I can tell," replied Tawzel, "wait here a moment."

For a short time, Tawzel flew much higher and then came swooping back down again, landing majestically with wings and tail feathers spread out. Her taloned feet barely made a sound as she landed on the grass.

Tawzel continued, "I am sorry to say that a few miles ahead of you there is a large road with many of the human machines on it. I can't see any way around it, and it will be very difficult to cross."

"Hm, thanks for letting us know," replied Rufous. "Just when we think we are making good progress we have something to slow us down. We will find a way to get across. Come on Piccola, let us see if we can get across before dawn."

"Good luck", Tawzel called out as she flew up into the night sky.

Rufous and Piccola headed off in the direction of the potentially dangerous obstacle ahead of them.

Having walked through a grassy field and over the brow of a hill they could see a large road a few hundred metres ahead of them, on which many vehicles travelled from left and right, their lights twinkling brightly - some lights were white while others were red. The road stretched for as far as the eye could see in both directions.

The two foxes paused, momentarily mesmerised by the sight.

Snapping out of it, Rufous said, "We have to stick close together."

"Okay," replied Piccola. "I don't like the look of this."

"It will be difficult to get across but if we are careful, and fast, then we can manage it. There is no other way around it."

"Okay," replied Piccola, unsure as to what to say.

They headed onwards towards the road.

As they neared the large road, they came across a tall chain link fence that looked to be impossible to get over or through.

Piccola and Rufus searched for a way under the fence. They looked to and fro until Piccola found a small opening.

"Here," she called to Rufus. "It's quite small, but I think we can get through."

Rufous sniffed around the opening and then started scratching and digging with his front claws. "I think rabbits have used this," he said. "It's a bit small, but with a little bit of work, we should be able to get under it."

"I wish we didn't have to cross the road," said Piccola. "But I suppose we don't have any other choice."

"No, we don't," replied Rufus.

Rufous scratched away for several minutes, and then he crept down and squeezed his way through the opening. He looked through the fence at Piccola, who was still standing on the other side. She looked uncertain as to whether she wanted to travel any further. Her eyes glistened in the dark.

"Come on," Rufus said. "It's not so bad."

Rufous looked at Piccola and sensing her caution, looked into her eyes and said, "I need you to come with me. It will be okay, we just need to stick close together."

"I just feel scared," replied Piccola.

Rufous tried to reassure Piccola, "Trust me, we can do this."

Although Piccola was frightened, she relented and crawled under the fence. As she squeezed through, she felt a sharp part of the fence catch the fur on her back, but she persisted and was soon standing next to Rufous.

"Are you okay?" asked Rufous.

"Yes," replied Piccola, "let's go."

They both walked slowly through the undergrowth of long grass towards the noisy traffic. As they reached the edge of the road, vehicles sped past them - from the left and the right.

For what seemed like an age, but was only a short time, they stood half-mesmerised by the sight. The cars' bright headlights lit the road in front of them, leaving an interval of momentary darkness before the next beams of light lit the road. As they went by, the red rear lights signified that the danger from each vehicle had passed.

"I don't think we can get across," stammered Piccola, her voice quivering with fear.

Rufous carried on watching studiously.

Rufous replied calmly, "I think we can, we just have to wait until the road goes dark. If we are quick I am sure we can make it. We have to sprint as fast as we can. There is no other way."

"I don't like it, I'm frightened," replied Piccola.

"It will be okay," Rufous replied, "we just need to stick together and run as fast as we can."

"Okay," Piccola said, but only half-believing it.

They crept closer to the edge of the road where there was a white line, some of the cars slowed down and Rufous sensed that the humans were looking at them.

Suddenly, the loud sound of a car horn blasted out just as it passed them. They briefly cowered down, unsure as to what would happen next.

The columns of vehicles continued one after another, with an occasional break in the line of traffic. When a lorry rumbled past they felt vibrations throughout their bodies.

Rufus watched intently, waiting for a large enough gap in the oncoming traffic. Most vehicles seemed to be traveling at the same speed, but he couldn't be sure. He looked further down the road, trying to predict when an opening would occur.

"Get ready," Rufous called out to Piccola. He could see a larger-than-normal gap about to appear in front of them.

"When I say run, just run to the other side as fast as you can, and DON'T stop!"

"Okay."

"RUN!" shouted Rufous, and they both ran in between the oncoming traffic. Rufous was to the right and slightly ahead of Piccola.

It wasn't far to sprint but their hearts were pounding.

The speeding cars had started to slow down and in a moment they were half-way across. It was then that Piccola trod on something sharp - a piece of broken glass - her front right paw sent a stinging pain to her brain. It caused her to slow slightly.

When Rufous reached the other side he hadn't realised that Piccola had slowed down. She was nearly there and to safety when the red car hit her. It knocked her up in the air and she landed on the side of the road on the grass verge - not moving.

Rufous paused and looked to his left where he could see his friend lying motionless, with blood trickling from her mouth.

Rufous went to Piccola's side and he sniffed her, nudged her, and spoke quietly to her.

"What have I done? I should have listened to you

Rufous lay down next to his friend as life started slowly seep away from her.

Without Rufous noticing, a car had stopped next to the two foxes and a human had got out and was looking at them.

Rufous was beyond caring, he looked at the hum: and then at his friend. He rested his head on Piccola's back. His heart was breaking more and more by the minute.

The human got back into their car but the car didn't move.

Time passed and while Piccola wasn't moving, Rufous could feel her faint heartbeat - but she didn't move.

Rufous didn't know how long he had been lying there, but suddenly he became aware of another person standing next to them.

Instinct told Rufous to step back away from the human and he reluctantly got up and moved a few metres away.

The human put their hands on Piccola, speaking quietly while they did this. They then went back to their vehicle, returning with a blanket which they placed over her.

They then picked Piccola up and started to carry her away. Rufous snarled in anguish, pacing backwards and forwards.

The human carried Piccola to their vehicle and then came back carrying a long stick with a metal hoop on the end of it. Rufous was frantic, he ran over to see where his friend was but he couldn't see her. As he turned around, the human had put the hoop around his neck and tightened it. He was trapped and he couldn't breathe properly. He had no means of escape.

Suddenly, the human grabbed Rufous by his back and lifted him into the back of the vehicle, into a small cage. At that moment, the metal noose was removed.

In the back of the vehicle where it was dimly lit, Rufous could just about see that in another cage, Piccola was lying motionless. He couldn't see if she was breathing.

Somewhere in the distance, Rufous could hear the 'KEEWIK, KEEWIK' of Tawzel.

After a short time, the vehicle started moving. Rufous could feel his heart racing, humans could never be trusted.

Rufous became overwhelmed by sadness. Why hadn't he listened to Piccola? When he had feared danger before, it was Piccola who had ignored him. It was a harsh lesson to learn, that sometimes you just had to trust your friends. Now it was too late.

After a short while the vehicle stopped moving and the rear doors were opened. Partly covered in a blanket, Piccola was carried silently away. Through the rear opening, Rufous could see the lights of a building.

After a short while, a different human came out and picked up the cage that Rufous was in, carrying him towards the building. Rufous looked around and could see lights everywhere, but there was no sign of Piccola.

They entered the building and Rufous could smell not just the scent of humans but also the scent of other animals. He could also smell death.

The cage was placed against another larger cage, and Rufous could see that an opening had appeared and he jumped through into the larger space. There was food and water in one corner and Rufous ate ferociously, drinking water when he had finished eating.

On the floor, there was some softer material in one corner and Rufous lay down on it. He felt so tired, but he couldn't stop thinking about Piccola and what had happened to her.

After a short while, Rufous fell asleep, woken intermittently by the screeching of an anguished animal.

Daylight arrived and Rufous paced around the cage. Slightly less fearful for his life, he had no idea where he was and what would become of him. Maybe like Piccola, he would be released and then set upon by hounds.

Throughout the day, different humans would come by his cage. One of them gave him food and spoke to him. Their voice was soft and Rufous cocked his head to one side to listen, while his ears twitched.

Chapter 9

Reunited

Several days passed by. The memory of Piccola being hit by the car and lying motionless was never far from Rufous's mind. He felt sad beyond words. Each day a human would come and usher him into an adjacent space, cleaning his cage and providing him with food and water.

On the fifth day, it was raining heavily. Rufous could hear the sound of the raindrops on the roof above. One of the humans came and crouched down next to Rufous's cage, talking softly to him. He wished he could understand what they were saying.

They stopped speaking and walked away.

A few minutes later the human reappeared, this time carrying a cage, and in the cage, there was Piccola, with a white bandage around one of her front legs. She looked towards Rufous and they both felt so happy to see each other.

The cage was put down next to Rufous's and after a moment, the two of them were reunited.

Piccola wasn't able to move very quickly but Rufous was so overwhelmed that he ran around Piccola excitedly. "I thought I had lost you," said Rufous, as he sniffed and licked his friend.

"I was in so much pain," replied Piccola. "I was asleep most of the time having vivid dreams of running across a road. When I woke up I couldn't move and now I am here!"

"Yes," replied Rufous. "I wonder what they will do with us now."

"I don't know," replied Piccola, "but they have been kind to me in helping me to recover."

"Yes," replied Rufous, "I thought you had been killed. I was so sad, but now I can be happy again. We must listen to each other when we fear danger!"

"Yes," replied Piccola, "we must."

As they continued sniffing each other, the human, who had stayed to watch them, said something. Piccola walked to the edge of the cage and sniffed the scent of the human. While Rufous looked on warily, Piccola felt safe and at ease. The human continued to talk softly to Piccola, and then the human walked away, leaving the two foxes alone.

Piccola suddenly felt a pang of hunger and she ate what was left in the food bowl.

The excitement of the moment had tired the two them and they curled up together on the soft floor and were soon asleep.

Many days passed. Piccola had regained her strength and the bandage had been removed from her leg. The two foxes had become restless, not knowing what was going to happen to them.

One evening, when dusk had already fallen, two humans came and ushered the foxes into two small cages. They were then carried into the back of a van. Th van's engine roared into life and the vehicle was transporting them to an unknown destination.

"Where do you think they are taking us?" asked Piccola.

"I don't know," replied Rufous. "I didn't like bein locked up, we may have been safe but I like to be outsid in nature."

"Yes," replied Piccola.

Their hearts were pounding as they contemplated what the future might hold for them. The sounds of many vehicles could be heard as they travelled along for what seemed a long time.

The van slowed down as it drove along an uneven surface which made it difficult for the foxes to keep their balance. The noise of traffic subsided into the distance and when the van stopped and the engine was turned off, there was the relative silence of nature, with the sounds from a busy road some distance behind them.

The rear doors of the van were opened and the two humans picked up Rufous's and Piccola's cages and placed them into a clearing of grass. The sky above was scattered with stars and the moon shone brightly.

Rufous looked skyward trying to work out which direction was east. Piccola looked around cautiously.

"What are they going to do with us?" asked Piccola.

"I don't know," replied Rufous, "I can't hear any hounds or horses."

The two humans stood by the van, talking quietly and watching the two foxes.

After a short while, the two humans walked over and stood by the two cages. At the same time, they bent down and opened each cage door. They then went and stood by the van.

At first, Rufous and Piccola seemed unsure as to what to do, but after a few seconds, they both darted ou of their cages and ran as fast as they could into the long grass. From behind them, they heard the humans call out. They didn't stop and just kept running.

After a few minutes, they were under the cover of trees.

"We are safe," said Piccola.

"Yes," replied Rufous.

Sounding relieved, Piccola said, "I can't hear any hounds

"No, neither can I," Rufous replied.

"The humans were kind to us," continued Piccola. "One of their machines nearly killed me, but then they helped me get better."

"I don't understand humans," replied Rufous. "One day some of them try to kill us and the next day another one helps us."

"I don't understand either," replied Piccola.

"To be safe, I think we must always treat humans as a threat," said Rufous.

"You are probably right," replied Piccola.

"We can continue on our journey now," replied Rufous. Looking up at the sky he continued, "I think this way is east."

"Okay," replied Piccola, "let's go."

As they walked slowly through the darkened woodland, above them came the sound of "KEEWIK, KEEWIK". It was Tawzel. She swooped down and landed on a branch near them.

"Here you are!" called out Tawzel. "I thought you had gone forever. I saw you by the road and watched as you were taken away. I stayed around here not knowing which way to go. And now you are back!"

"Hi Tawzel," Rufous and Piccola said together.

"It's a long story," continued Rufous, but the humans helped Piccola to get better, and then brought us back here. We are going to continue travelling east, will you come with us?"

"Yes, I would like that," said Tawzel, "maybe some woodland and fields where we can live together and be safe."

"Yes, that would be good," replied Rufous. Even if we can't get home, maybe we can find somewhere safe."

"The large road is behind us and ahead there are many fields and woodland," replied Tawzel.

"That sounds good," replied Piccola.

"Okay, let's go," said Rufous.

"Hurray!" Tawzel called out in joy, as she flew up into the darkness.

Rufous and Piccola followed along, occasionally looking skyward to try to see or hear their friend. The stars in the sky seemed to twinkle extra brightly as they continued once again on their journey.

Printed in Great Britain
by Amazon

34208276R00059